I G A N

Norwood

CATHEAD POINT

NORTH MANITOU
ISLAND

Northport
Point

Northport   Northport   Eastport
Bay

SOUTH MANITOU
ISLAND

Grand

Omena

Traverse

Bay

Leland

Peshawbestown

Suttons Bay   Old
Mission

PYRAMID POINT   Lake Leelanau

Sleeping Bear   Lake

Kewadino

Bay   LEELANAU

West Arm

Glen Arbor   Leelanau

Elk Rapids

SLEEPING BEAR   Glen
Lake

Mapleton

East Arm

Burdickville   Maple   Cedar
City

Empire   Rennie

Bates

Greilickville

Traverse City   GRAND

Acme

Lake Ann   Long L.

Platte
Lake

Crystal
Lake   Honor   Interlochen   Grawn

Frankfort   BENZIE   Duck L.

Boardman

Beulah   Bendon   TRAVERSE

Elberta   Benzonia   Monroe Cen.   Mayfield

Green   Hannah
L.
Wallin   Karlin   Kingsley
Summit City

Thompsonville   C&O   Nessen City   Walt

Arcadia   Copemish   Buckley
Pomona

The Legend *of* Sleeping Bear

By Kathy-jo Wargin
Illustrations by Gijsbert van Frankenhuyzen

Sleeping Bear Press
121 South Main
P.O. Box 20
Chelsea, MI 48118
www.sleepingbearpress.com

Printed and bound in Canada by Friesens, Altona, Manitoba.

10 9 8 7 6 5 4 3

Cataloging-in-Publication Data on file.   ISBN 1-886947-35-X

The great bear sleeps - - waiting for
her cubs - - who have turned into the Manitou
Islands - - the wind sweeps on.

The story of their trip across Lake
Michigan has become a legend for young and
old - - which is dedicated to your imagination
and fantasy that you may enjoy it forever and
ever - - - as the wind blows - - -

Gwen Frostic

For all mothers, whose love and dedication will be rewarded.

A Legend

A legend is a story created about a certain person or place. Many legends are created as a way of explaining history. Most legends are based in fiction, which means that they are not necessarily true. However, the real magic of a legend exists in the fact that it is a story passed on from generation to generation.

In writing **The Legend of Sleeping Bear**, it was my goal to remind people why this legend is so meaningful, and to introduce new generations to the beauty and symbolism that lives on through the Sleeping Bear Dunes National Lakeshore.

Here is my version of the legend, and may the legend live on in your heart.

Kathy-jo Wargin

Long, long ago,
before voyageurs paddled canoes down
rivers and streams, before mighty lumbermen
cleared forests with sharp, shiny axes,

before wooden ships carried sailors
across great freshwater seas,

there was a beautiful forest near the edge of a mighty lake.

Today, we know that forest as part of Wisconsin, and the mighty lake is called Lake Michigan.

But this was a time before many
places had names or people.
It was a time before farmers and
Native Americans planted cherry and
apple trees in long, neat rows.
It was a time before pioneers planted colorful
gardens of pumpkins, potatoes, and corn.

In this forest near the edge of the lake lived
Mother Bear. Her fur was blacker than the darkest night,
and her eyes were large and round.

Mother Bear had two cubs, and they were very soft and playful. The three of them lived together in a small, cozy den nestled among bluebells and buttercups.

Every morning, as the wood thrush softly
sang pip-pip-pip, and chickadees called
chick-a-dee-dee-dee from the trees,

Mother Bear and her cubs would lumber through the forest
to the banks of the birch-lined stream.

Deer would gently bend their slender necks to sip the cool water, and raccoons would quickly wash their faces. Mother Bear and her cubs would step carefully into the stream, and as the fresh, clear, water trickled by, Mother Bear would teach her cubs how to snatch plump, colorful trout for breakfast.

Afterward, they would sit lazily
on the banks, nibbling blueberries
and hazelnuts.

Every afternoon, Mother Bear would lead her cubs through the forest to the edge of the mighty lake. This lake was so big they could not see the other side, and the water seemed to disappear into the sky.

The bears would frolic along the sandy shore, happily splashing in the shallows and chasing herring gulls. They tugged at each other's tails, and took long, cool baths.

Every evening, Mother Bear led her cubs back to their warm cozy den where she cradled them in her big black paws and held them gently while they went to sleep.

One morning, as they were lumbering along to the birch-lined stream, there was a loud crash of thunder and a sharp, hissing sound!

Snap! Pop!

Mother Bear stood on her hind feet and stuck her nose in the air. A brilliant orange blaze flashed through the trees, and dark clouds filled the sky...

...Fire!

Mother Bear rushed her cubs to the
banks of the stream, and ordered them to
follow it to the shore of the mighty lake.

Bears dashed rapidly,
deer sprang back and forth,
and wolves ran wildly.

Even the star-nosed moles hurried out from
beneath the cover of the forest floor.

As they reached the shore, Mother Bear
gathered her cubs and shouted,
"Children, we must go!
We must swim across the mighty lake,
my children, I love you so!"

They leaped into the water and began to swim.
The lake was very deep. The water was cold.
The waves were tall and the wind was strong.
They paddled hard and fast.

Mother Bear pleaded,
"My children, do you promise
that you'll swim with all your might?
If we are to reach the other side,
we must swim throughout the night!"

The faithful cubs promised their mother that they would swim with all of their might.

They swam and they swam, growing weary and tired. They swam as the afternoon sun grew large and warm. They swam as the sun slipped below the horizon and the air grew cold.

And as they swam, Mother Bear kept turning her large, black face to make sure her cubs were not far behind. She watched as their paws struggled against the water. And as their soft round faces became smaller and smaller between the waves of the mighty lake, Mother Bear grew worried.

Soon, nighttime fell upon them. The sky grew dark, and stars began to shine. Suddenly, the air seemed quiet and the water became very still. In the distance, Mother Bear heard the trill of screech owls and the howling of timber wolves.

Mother Bear kept looking back as she swam throughout the night. Through her tired eyes, she noticed the morning sun was beginning to rise and cast its bright rays upon the deep blue water.

She looked back once more but could not see her cubs.

Mother Bear collapsed on the banks of the
shore. Her wet, heavy paws sank into the deep
sand. There were rolling hills and huge
mounds of sand all around her, and the land
seemed very strange.

Mother Bear paced up and down the water's edge, but her cubs were nowhere to be found. Her wet fur gleamed in the fresh morning sunlight, and tears shone in her eyes.

Mother Bear cried,
"My children, are you coming?
You are strong, and you are clever!
My children, can you hear me?
I will wait for you forever."

Mother Bear climbed to the top of the highest hill.
She looked out over the dark, deep water,
but saw no sign of her cubs.

Mother Bear called throughout the day,
"My children, can you hear me?
I know you must be near!
My children, I am waiting,
waiting high up here."

Mother Bear waited until the sun set and another night
fell upon her. She waited while the sun
came up again in the morning.

She waited while wild pink roses bloomed all around her and while baby white-throated sparrows learned how to fly. She waited while the grasses on the distant dune became yellow and dull.

She waited while the leaves fell from the beech trees.

Mother Bear waited while the air grew colder
and snowflakes floated down
from thick, dark winter clouds.

She waited. And waited. Mother Bear waited, but her cubs never reached the shore.

And high upon the hill, Mother Bear fell fast asleep in her sorrow. Years passed, and the winds of Lake Michigan blew blankets of sand upon her, keeping her warm and safe in her slumber.

Over time, the great spirit of the land felt her sadness, recognizing her dedication and love for her children. With a tremendous gust of wind, the spirit brought the cubs near shore, raising them out of the water as two magnificent islands, placing them forever within the watchful and caring eyes of Mother Bear.

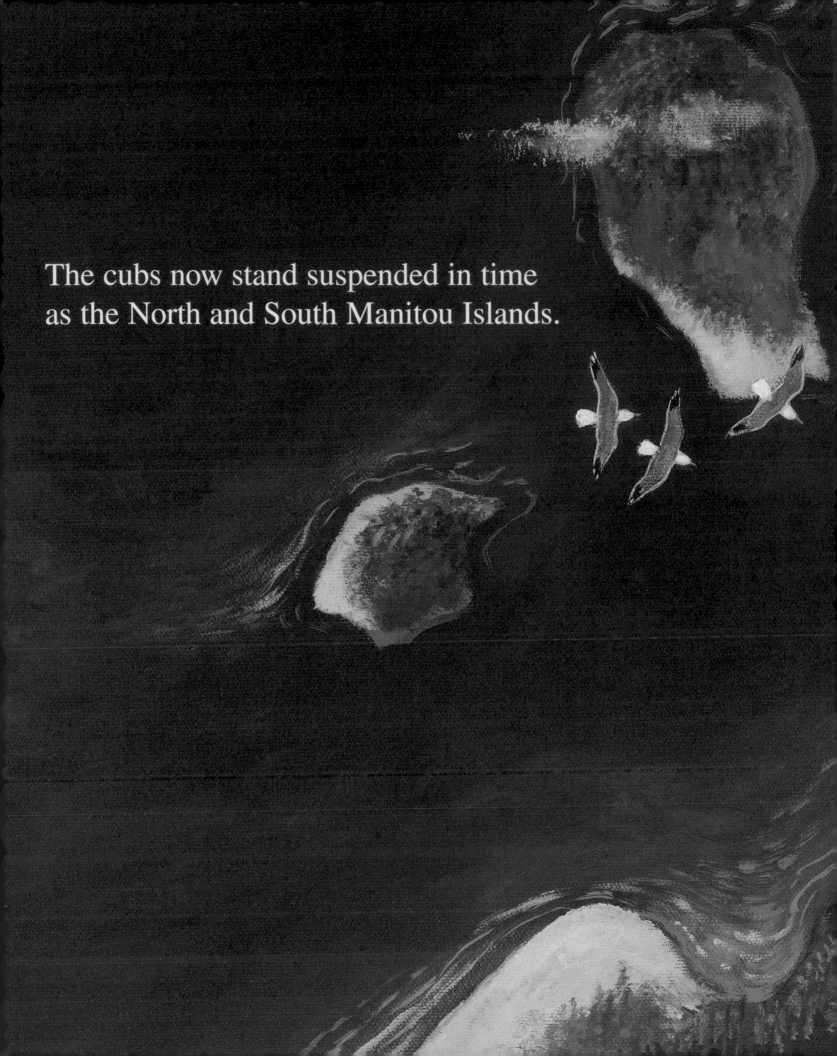

The cubs now stand suspended in time
as the North and South Manitou Islands.

Happy to be near their mother once again,
they rest in the spirit of their mother's love;
two islands of gleaming sand edged by
waters that sparkle and dance in the sunlight.

Now, Mother Bear can finally rest with great happiness, knowing her cubs are near. And today, when the world is quiet and the sun begins to set, you can still hear her voice echoing in the wind that blows across Lake Michigan.

My children, as the years may pass,
and time slips through our hands,
my love will linger near the shore
and in the blowing sands.

I'll send you kisses in the wind
to let you know I'm here,
sleeping near the water's edge,
I am always near.

My children, you can rest assured,
that we are now together,
and I am watching over you,
and loving you forever.

Gijsbert van Frankenhuyzen

The art of Gijsbert van Frankenhuyzen captures his lifelong connection to nature and wildlife. Brimming with passionate details and brilliant color, his paintings have been published in several books. His talent for mural painting can be seen in several Michigan museums, including Fort Mackinac on Mackinac Island, Michigan.

Born in The Netherlands, Gijsbert studied at the Royal Academy of Arts and immigrated to the United States in 1976. In 1993, after 17 years as the Art Director for the *Michigan Natural Resources Magazine,* he ventured out on his own as an artist and educator.

His highest professional achievement comes from being selected numerous times into the internationally renowned Leigh Yawkey Woodson *Birds in Art* exhibition. Traveling to schools in the Midwest, Gijsbert shares his love of painting and wildlife rehabilitation. Gijsbert and his wife Robbyn, give nature tours at their home in Bath, Michigan, outside Lansing, where they live with their two daughters, Kelly and Heather.

Kathy-jo Wargin

As the author of many poems and stories for children, Kathy-jo Wargin aims to help young readers notice the most intricate details of a story by adding the nuances that create magic and wonder in a good tale.

Born and raised in northern Minnesota, her love of pine-filled forests and glistening lakes inspired her pursuit of writing. Now, with more than a decade of experience as a professional writer, her collection of published works includes poetry and nonfiction.

Recently, she and her husband, photographer Ed Wargin, along with their son Jake, traveled extensively throughout Michigan completing a travel guide titled *Scenic Driving Michigan.*